To Elia, who has a Santa Claus
all to herself!
To Ronan and his gift drawings!
N. C.

To Arsene.
R. B.

From the same authors:
All the Things a Teacher Will Never Say
ISBN: 978-0-7643-6218-7

Copyright © 2021 by Schiffer Publishing, Ltd.

Translated from French by Simulingua, Inc.

Originally published as *Tout ce que le pere Noel ne fera Jamais* © 2018 © L'Élan vert, Saint-Pierre-des-Corps

Library of Congress Control Number: 2020952759

Cover design by Jack Chappell
Type set in GedProvidence/Infant

ISBN: 978-0-7643-6217-0
Printed in China

Published by Schiffer Kids
An imprint of Schiffer Publishing, Ltd.
4880 Lower Valley Road
Atglen, PA 19310
Phone: (610) 593-1777; Fax: (610) 593-2002
E-mail: Info@schifferbooks.com
Web: www.schifferbooks.com

For our complete selection of fine books on this and related subjects, please visit our website at www.schifferbooks.com. You may also write for a free catalog.

Schiffer Publishing's titles are available at special discounts for bulk purchases for sales promotions or premiums. Special editions, including personalized covers, corporate imprints, and excerpts, can be created in large quantities for special needs. For more information, contact the publisher.

All the Things SANTA CLAUS Will Never Do

Noé Carlain

Ronan Badel

Schiffer **Kids**™

4880 Lower Valley Road, Atglen, PA 19310

Write a letter to himself asking for gifts.

Sing "O Christmas Tree" in front of every Christmas tree and be late delivering toys.

Forget his suspenders—watch out!
Too late: he lost his pants . . .

Stop to play hide-and-seek with the reindeer in the forest when the sleigh is ready.

Take a long nap on Christmas Eve and forget to wake up on time.

Put a bow on his head and become a present instead
of leaving presents.

Cross a field with a bull in it, wearing his beautiful red suit.

Take a selfie with his reindeer.

Confuse Easter with Christmas.

Forget to take his GPS and get really lost.

Remove his boots so his elves can smell his stinky cheese toes.

Unwrap the presents and play with them . . .

Pull the sleigh himself because
his reindeer are tired.

Forget to wish Merry Christmas to Mrs. Claus and their seven children.

Crash into trees because he doesn't
even have his flying license.

Eat all the cookies left by the children and no longer fit through the chimney.

Yeah! Cool! Deliver the presents on a skateboard for a change. What?

Get the presents mixed up—what a shock
for Grandma not to get a hat for her collection!

But what Santa Claus would never, ever do . . .

. . . He would never forget where you live!

Because he knows you're the real gift at Christmastime.